THE MONSTER WHO DID MY MATH

WRITTEN BY
DANNY SCHNITZLEIN

ILLUSTRATED BY
BILL MAYER

Ω
PEACHTREE
ATLANTA

There once was a time I was frightened by numbers.
They scared me at school, and they haunted my slumbers.
My brain had some kind of allergic reaction
To multiplication...addition...subtraction.

My blood would run cold at the thought of division
And decimal points would put spots in my vision.
But now I see math from a new point of view.
This is my story. I swear it's all true.

It was late on a Sunday—and long past my bath.
I'd waited all weekend to work on my math.
I opened the book, and my hands started shaking.

My forehead was sweating. My stomach was aching.
My vision went blurry. I wanted to run.
"If only," I cried, "all this homework were done!"

The clock chimed a warning with twelve hollow tones.

My spine began tingling. A chill froze my bones.

Outside in the yard, lightning flashed with a *boom,*

And a creature took shape in my shadowy room.
His horns were bright red and his cape midnight black,
And his pencilly fingers tapped "clickety-clack."

"Boo hoo," growled the monster. "I'm feeling your pain.
This awful arithmetic's draining your brain.
Say *hasta luego* to multiplication.

Forget your subtraction. Go take a vacation!
It's fast and it's painless...and all guaranteed.
Just sign on the line, and you'll get what you need."

I signed as he sharpened his fingers and thumbs.

He added the addends and figured their sums.

He gave me my copy and raised one eyebrow.

"Pay later?" he asked me, "or settle up now?"
"Later!" I answered. He laughed long and deep.
In a flash he was gone, and I went right to sleep.

At school Monday morning, my homework was praised.
The answers were perfect! My teacher, amazed!

My problems were solved—in more ways than one—
And no one but me could say how it was done.

I looked at my homework that night—tons of graphing.
I called for the monster. He couldn't stop laughing.
"You kids of today are pathetic and lazy.

Your minds are all mooshy. Your morals are hazy."
He graphed all the points, then he figured my bill.
"I'll pay later," I said, and he growled, "Yes, you will."

The teacher looked over my work the next day.
I couldn't believe it. She gave me an A!
But then Mrs. Markov said, "Come to the board."
She wrote an equation. My temperature soared.

My guts did a skydive. My knobby knees knocked.
My classmates were giggling. The clock ticked and tocked.
I prayed I might vanish like some kind of ghost.
The teacher was fuming. My hiney was toast.

I called that old creep when I got home from school.
"You burned me!" I told him. "I felt like a fool!"
He rolled out my contract and showed the fine print.

"Look here," said the monster. "You might need to squint.
In paragraph seven of clause ninety-three,
'If *you* don't learn anything, do not blame *me!*'"

My blood began boiling. My cheeks turned bright red.
"Hit the road! Take a hike! Don't come back here!" I said.
"I'll go," snarled the monster. "There's just one more thing...
Your bill comes to sixty-four dollars. Cha-CHING!"

I busted my bank, and he snatched up my money.
He counted and snickered. I asked, "What's so funny?"
"Your total is lacking by two fifty-two.
Your math needs improvement. But what else is new?"

I tore up my room in the quest for more cash.

Three pennies plinked out when I dumped out the trash.

Down deep in my dresser, I dug out a buck.

Two quarters turned up in a shoebox. What luck!

I did some addition and added the stuff.

Only one fifty-three. It wasn't enough.

How much would I need to complete the transaction?

I picked up my pencil and did some subtraction.

From two fifty-two I took one fifty-three.

Just ninety-nine cents and I'd finally be free!

Way down in the hamper, eight nickels were shining.

I fished out six dimes from my winter coat lining.

My change came to forty, plus sixty cents more.

My heart thumped and jumped as I totaled the score.

All the money was there, with a penny to spare!
I cheered and did cartwheels. I jumped in the air.
He flipped me a penny and shredded my bill.
He left snarling, "Call me. You know that you will!"

My homework that night was on decimal places.
I opened the book and made horrible faces.
I pulled out some paper and worked problem one
With the hint of a grin. Could it be? Was this fun?
As I worked problem two, I was starting to think

For the very first time, "Maybe math doesn't stink!"
Then, deep in the shadows, I sensed someone lurking.
I knew who it was, so I kept right on working.
"YOU NEED ME!" he bellowed. He thundered and roared.
But the louder he got, well, the more I ignored.

And while I was carefully writing and thinking,
I couldn't believe it. That monster was shrinking!
The more I kept working, the smaller he got
Till he shrank to the size of a wee little dot.
I glanced at the guy, just a miniscule speck.

Then I looked at my homework and said, "What the heck."
I scooped him right up. I can still see his face.
And I dropped him right down in a decimal point's place—
The point in the middle of 7.9.
I smooshed him down flat, and he stuck there just fine.

I finished my homework and climbed into bed,
Remembering something the monster had said:
"If you don't pay up front, you'll pay later instead."

And though that old monster was far from a friend,

And his service is one that I can't recommend,

He did make a very good point...

        ...in the end.

To my better ¹/₂ Kerry, who helps everything add up right
—D. S.

For Forest,
remember all of the zeros in the world still add up to zero.
—B. M.

Ω

Published by
PEACHTREE PUBLISHERS
1700 Chattahoochee Avenue
Atlanta, Georgia 30318-2112
www.peachtree-online.com

Text © 2007 by Danny Schnitzlein
Illustrations © 2007 by Bill Mayer

Book and cover design by Bill Mayer and Loraine M. Joyner
Composition by Melanie McMahon Ives

The illustrations were produced by dipping a tranquilized squid into small vats of liquefied, colored chalks and randomly applying him (or was it her?) to pencil sketches on carrot paper. Then hairbrushing (airbrushed gouache, dyes and digital). The words were produced in the usual way. Text typeset in International Typeface Corporation's Stone Serif; title created in Rob Villareal's Danzig 4p (Ravenous Media); back cover fonts are Blazing, Ray Larabie's Green Fuz (Larabie Fonts), Pete Dombrezian's Dom Bold (Bitstream), Monotype Imaging's Maiandra, Adobe's Helvetica Boldface Condensed, and International Typeface Corporation's Stone Serif.

Printed and manufactured in April 2010 by Imago in Singapore
10 9 8 7 6 5 4 3

Library of Congress Cataloging-in-Publication Data

Schnitzlein, Danny.
 The monster who did my math / written by Danny Schnitzlein ; illustrated by Bill Mayer. -- 1st ed.
   p. cm.
 Summary: When a monster offers to help a boy who is afraid of numbers by doing his math homework, the boy eagerly signs a contract and agrees to pay later, but the first time he is asked to solve a problem in class and cannot, he realizes he has gotten no bargain.
 ISBN 13: 978-1-56145-420-4
 ISBN 10: 1-56145-420-6
 [1. Math anxiety--Fiction. 2. Mathematics--Fiction. 3. Monsters--Fiction. 4. Humorous stories. 5. Stories in rhyme.] I. Mayer, Bill, ill. II. Title.
PZ8.3.S2972Mod 2007
[E]--dc22
                    2006103228

For my girls, I love you big!

— K.G.

For Junie and Jalen.
You are Truly fierce and fabulous!

— A.R.

Library of Congress Cataloging-in-Publication Data • Names: Greenawalt, Kelly, author. | Rauscher, Amariah, illustrator. • Title: Princess Truly in I am Truly / by Kelly Greenawalt ; illustrated by Amariah Rauscher. • Other titles: I am Truly • Description: First edition. | New York : Orchard Books, an imprint of Scholastic Inc., 2017. | Summary: "Princess Truly's rhyming adventures are a celebration of individuality, girl power, diversity, and dreaming big!"—Provided by publisher. • Identifiers: LCCN 2016050195 (print) | LCCN 2017004676 (ebook) | ISBN 9781338167207 (hardcover : alk. paper) ISBN 9781338184907 • Subjects: | CYAC: Stories in rhyme. | Princesses—Fiction. • Classification: LCC PZ8.3.G7495 Pr 2017 (print) | LCC PZ8.3.G7495 (ebook) | DDC [E]—dc23 • LC record available at https://lccn.loc.gov/2016050195

10 9 8 7 6 5 4 3 2 1   17 18 19 20 21 • Printed in the U.S.A.   88 • First edition, August 2017
Book design by Patti Ann Harris

Princess Truly
in
I Am Truly

by
Kelly Greenawalt

illustrated by
Amariah Rauscher

Orchard Books
An Imprint of Scholastic Inc.
New York

I am Truly.

I like frogs
and the color blue.
I can climb trees
and be a rock star, too.

I can run fast
and build tall towers.

I am a superhero
with magical powers.

I am smart,

I am studious,

I am a high achiever.

I am strong,
I am skillful,
I am a born leader.

I can sail the seas
on a little boat.
I can eat every bite
of a root beer float.

I can tie
my own shoes.
I can find treasure
with clues.

I am clever,
I am curious,
I am an engineer.

I am confident,
I am courageous,
I am a volunteer.

 I can fly to the moon

and dance on the stars.

I can tame wild lions
and race fast cars.

I can swim like a fish.
I can shoot and swish.

I am funny,
I am flexible,
I am an entertainer.

I am focused,
I am fierce,
I am a dinosaur trainer.

I can grow
purple grapes.
I can create
amazing shapes.

I can feed
hungry bunnies
crunchy carrots.

I can learn
Japanese
and teach it
to parrots.

I am Truly, watch me soar.
I am small but mighty,
hear me R R

I can do anything
I set my mind to do.

Do you know that you
can do all these things, too?

You are Truly Fabulous!

Dear Readers:

We created Princess Truly for our daughters. We wanted them to see a strong, smart, problem-solving, confident young girl with beautiful curls who could do anything she set her mind to! We hope these books inspire readers everywhere to reach for the stars, dream big, and stay TRUE to who they are.

Kelly

Amariah

Kelly and her daughters,
Calista and Kaia

Amariah with her daughters,
Jalen and Junie